Krista, Brian, and Baby Zaj[illegible]

Happy Reading!

Love, Ryan B.

Krista, Brian, and Baby Zajeskey -
Happy Reading!
Love, Ryan B.

What's So Bad About Being an Only Child?

Cari Best *Pictures by* Sophie Blackall

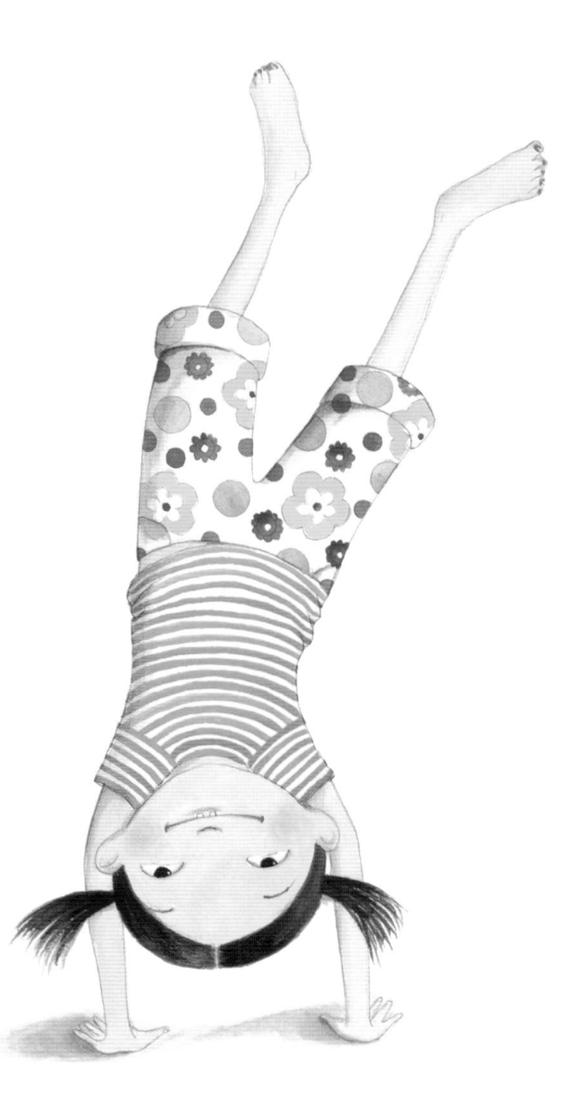

Melanie Kroupa Books
Farrar, Straus and Giroux ✿ New York

For members of the special O.C. Club: Sandy, Stephen, Margaret, Dennis, Alida, Jenna, Elliot, Brianne, Freddy, Laurie, Leslie, Sharon, David, Molly, Catherine, Rosemary, Francesca, Maria, Erica, Anya, Alisa, Melanie, Patrick, Michael, Maxine, Syed, Lisa, Robert, Sangeeta, Kelly, Jason, Courtney, Kate, Vivian, Paul, Joshua, Mabel, Joanne, Joe, Claire, Tim, Barbara, and 15 million more
—C.B.

For Imogen, Gloria, Luisa, Melanie, and Wallace
—S.B.

Distributed in Canada by Douglas & McIntyre Ltd.
Color separations by Chroma Graphics PTE Ltd.
Printed and bound in China by South China Printing Co. Ltd.
Designed by Jay Colvin
First edition, 2007
1 3 5 7 9 10 8 6 4 2

www.fsgkidsbooks.com

Library of Congress Cataloging-in-Publication Data
Best, Cari.
What's so bad about being an only child? / Cari Best ; pictures by Sophie Blackall.— 1st ed.
p. cm.
Summary: Rosemary Emma Angela Lynette Isabel Iris Malone grows tired of being an only child, but eventually finds a way to feel less alone.
ISBN-13: 978-0-374-39943-6
ISBN-10: 0-374-39943-3
[1. Only child—Fiction. 2. Family life—Fiction. 3. Pets—Fiction.] I. Blackall, Sophie, ill. II. Title.

PZ7.B46575 Wgr 2007
[E]—dc22

2005051232

Rosemary Emma Angela Lynette Isabel Iris Malone knew what it was like to be an only child.

She had a lot of experience.

ANGELA!
ROSEMARY!
EMM
IRIS!
LYNETTE!
ISABEL!

When she was born, no one could decide what to name her.
"Rosemary is *my* favorite name," said her mother.
"You mean Emma," said her father.
"We want Angela," said one set of grandparents.
"No. Lynette," said the other.
"Isabel or else," said Aunt Barbara.
"Iris or my name is mud," said Uncle Jeff.
So her parents gave her all six names and no one was insulted.

The new baby had a lot of admirers.

"She's so thoughtful," said her mother when she slept through the night.

"Hale and hearty," said her father when she squeezed his pointing finger.

"How coordinated!" said one set of grandparents when she started to creep and crawl.

"Very graceful," said the other set when she learned to wave goodbye.

"Good-humored, too," said Aunt Barbara when she laughed at all her jokes.

“And is she ever smart!” said Uncle Jeff when she said her first words, which were:

"I HATE HAVING ALL THOSE NAMES!"

So from then on, Rosemary Emma Angela Lynette Isabel Iris Malone was known simply as Rosemary because all her relatives wanted their only child to be happy.

At first, Rosemary *was* happy. She was the center of attention and the object of affection. "I am the honey in their hive," she gurgled.

For no sooner did Rosemary open her mouth than someone put food in it. When she complained about being wet, someone quickly made her dry. If she was bored, someone hurried over to play peekaboo or the piano or read to her from *Charlotte's Web*.

But sometimes all these things happened at once. And Rosemary was *not* happy.

"Being an only child is hard work," she said.

As she grew older, Rosemary wished she could escape.

But she couldn't. While her mother held one hand, her father held the other, and Rosemary had no hand left to hold her ice cream or fly her kite or even blow her nose.

This only-child business has got to stop, Rosemary thought.

Rosemary took her complaint all the way to her mother. “You need to have another kid right away,” she told her. “And that’s that.”

Her mother looked puzzled. So Rosemary said, “When I grow up, I’m going to have twenty-three children so no one will be an only child.”

“What’s so bad about being an only child?” asked her mother.

“*Everything!*” said Rosemary.

Her father tried to cheer her up by singing:

But it only made things worse.

"Everything is so easy and quiet and organized around here," she told him. "Can we please have another kid?"

Her father looked puzzled. So Rosemary said, "When I grow up, I'm not having *any* children, so no one will be an only child."

"What's so bad about being an only child?" asked her father.

"Everything!" said Rosemary.

All of Rosemary's friends had brothers and sisters. She longed to have a brother in the top bunk to play shipwreck with like her friend Sidney, or a sister like her friend Mona to share clothes and toys with and tell deep, dark secrets to. Even when Mona and her sister argued over who got to open the treasure chest, Rosemary felt it was like belonging to a special club. Only I'm not a member, she thought.

Rosemary invited her friends to spend the day at her house—and sometimes even the night. But in the end, everyone had to go home.

She dreamed about being someone's sister. She read stories about families and pretended she was part of the big family that lived in her dollhouse.

When she played checkers, she made believe that the red checkers were sisters and the black checkers were brothers.

On her wall she wrote:

I WANT TO BE SOMEONE'S SISTE

"or else . . ." she told her bear.

To make herself feel better, Rosemary started collecting "only" things—like a sock, a button, the last cookie on the plate, a wheel, and a plastic nose—so they wouldn't feel alone. Her family was beginning to worry.

Then one day, Rosemary, out exploring, discovered an interesting rock. An "only" rock. The rock moved. It was headed for the street. "Stop!" she yelled. But the rock didn't listen.

The rock was really a turtle, which Rosemary named Belle because it rhymed with shell, which was where Belle was hiding when Rosemary took her home.

"A turtle?" asked her parents.

"Winter is coming. Can she stay here?" asked Rosemary.

"Here?" asked her parents. "What do we want with a turtle?"

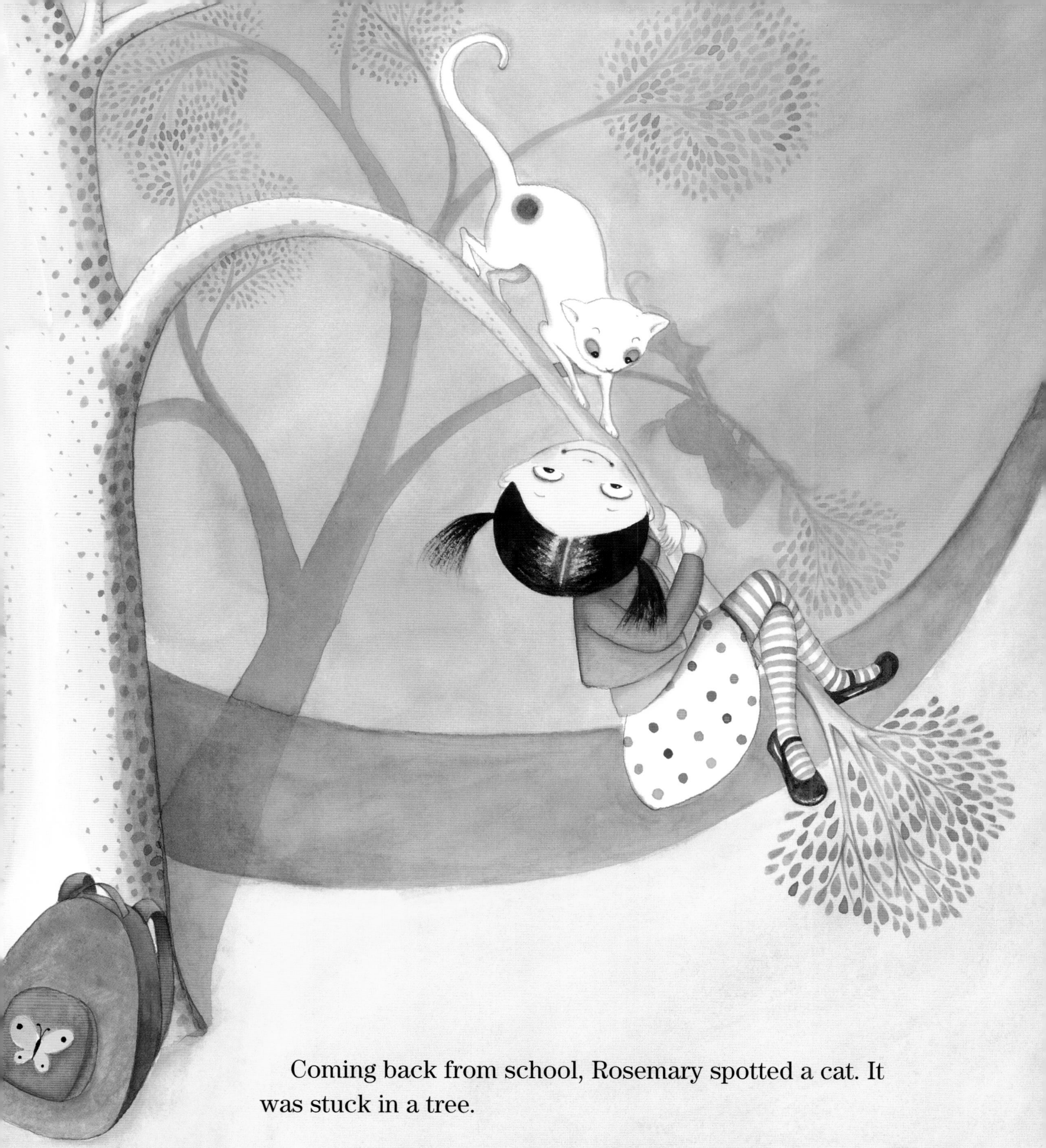

Coming back from school, Rosemary spotted a cat. It was stuck in a tree.

"A cat?" asked her parents.

"Her name is Dot. Can she stay here?" asked Rosemary.

"Here?" asked her parents. "What do we want with a cat?"

Next Rosemary found a rabbit. His name was Jack.
"A rabbit?" asked her parents.
"Sidney's allergic. Can he stay here?" asked Rosemary.
"Here?" asked her parents. Then they helped her build a hutch.

MIKE

Soon there was a dog.

"A dog?" asked her parents.

"He has no collar and he has no name," said Rosemary. So they helped her name him Mike.

After Belle and after Dot, after Jack and after Mike, Rosemary's family got two birds, Bo and Peep. The birds had babies. Then along came a spider named Charlotte and a pig named Wilbur.

They played shipwreck, ate cookies, argued, and shared secrets any time they wanted to. And no one had to go home, which made Rosemary very happy—

because although she was still an only child,
she hardly ever felt like one.

And that was the most important thing of all.